Claudia Haase

A Truthful Companion By My Side

FSC
www.fsc.org
MIX
Papier aus verantwortungsvollen Quellen
Paper from responsible sources
FSC® C105338

Bibliographic information of the German National Library: The German National Library lists this publication in the German National Bibliography; detailed bibliographic data is available on the Internet and can be accessed via http://dnb.dnb.de.

Cover: Cod Gray #9471, BookCoverZone.com
Design by Diren Yardimli
Editing and proofreading of the English Version: Sierra Campbell, Editing by Sierra

Published by: BoD · Books on Demand GmbH, Überseering 33, 22297 Hamburg, bod@bod.de

Printed by: Libri Plureos GmbH, Friedensallee 273, 22763 Hamburg

ISBN: 978-3-8192-7620-0

Contents

Chapter One

Bergfels Palace, 1712

Agatha

My eyelids are heavy, and it takes me a while to blink and embrace my surroundings. The morning sun shines in through the window and announces the dawn of a new day. *How grateful I am to be able to experience it!*

Even if I do not know whcther I will bc ablc to hold out until the evening. Only the fervent desire to say farewell to my beloved Ernestine has given me the strength not to hand myself over to Charon, the ferryman of death.

Tired of being upright, I seek to lie down, but my chambermaid, Yolande, is at hand in an instant.

"Your Highness, I told you to take care of yourself! Wait, I am coming to help!" Yolande whirls around the bed and stuffs countless cushions into my back so that I am a little more comfortable.

"You know that too much blood flows into your head when you lie down. It is unhealthy and can even lead to death," she reminds me reproachfully.

My vision is clouded, and I can only see the objects in the room, not recognize them. This is probably not only due to the lack of daylight in my room. Yolande's glowing red cheeks appear in front of me, her eyebrows raised. Concern is written all over her face.

I shiver, even though I can hear the cozy crinkling and crackling coming from the fireplace. Nevertheless, for a while, I thought I was at Sturmstein Castle with Ernestine, where there is a constant draft through all the cracks in the walls.

But no, I am in my bedchamber in Bergfels Palace. I saw the first light of day here not quite sixty-two years ago and will obviously be leaving this earth soon.

Memories creep up inside my head. Ernestine fanning me after dancing and showering me with all her love. Ernestine, who grinned mischievously and told me she had hidden a love letter to me in a gap in the castle walls. I think of our walks and rides together and how we talked intensively about music, literature, our horses... but I also recall the saddest time in my life, when my young friend was struggling with her fate and...

Oh, if I could turn back time! How I would love to float across the ballroom dance floor one last time with Stinchen, *as I call her in secret.*

Instead, I am dragged down by my tiredness that catches up to me.

Ernestine

This slow jerking is unbearable. More than thirty years ago, I would have shouted at the coachman to stop. I would have hopped out of the carriage and found a reason to make my travel companion dismount and move a few meters away from us. It is evil enough that my brother, Count Cuno, forced a chaperone on me!

In no time, I would have jumped into the saddle with my skirts ruffled and galloped across the country toward Bergfels Palace.

With my skirts ruffled? No, I would have snatched a pair of my brother's practical Rhinegrave breeches for the journey. They are much more suitable for riding.

Then I would have covered the distance to the palace in an instant. Even if I'd had to take a break due to the onset of dusk, I would have sneaked into a farmer's hayloft and left before dawn.

But my back is bothering me, and my knees are always giving me pain. According to Queen Blanchefleur, my sister, it's because I spent too much of my childhood running through the woods or jumping on horses. In addition, I should also stop eating so much, and in general, I should not forget that I have sinned all my life.

Those were the days when I roamed the woods without a care in the world! But now I need a proper bed to sleep in. Although I am a lot younger than Agatha, at my age, it's unthinkable to get out of the carriage without a helping hand. Especially with this puffy traveling dress that my sister recently talked me into purchasing. It is ideal for trips through the country and supposedly *le dernier cri,* the height of fashion, in its shape and color.

Now, my heart is broken. I am full of sorrow for my princess, my dearly beloved, who has accompanied me most of my life and stood by me in my most difficult hours. I hope and pray I will see my dearest Agatha alive.

A foolish argument, a difference of opinion, divided us a few weeks ago and I fled in anger to Cuno, my brother, to Sturmstein Castle. I wish I had gone to our grandparents' prestigious palace instead; God rest their souls! I would have reached Agatha much more quickly from there. A second cousin lives there these days, and she would certainly have taken me in.

How much I now regret having to travel such a great distance!

I force myself to think about something else, otherwise I will start crying again. And by all means, I do not want to face Agatha with reddened eyes. I want to be as flawlessly beautiful to her as I was on the first day we met.

Chapter Two

Thirty years earlier, in 1682

Ernestine

"Now take a look, Ernestine!"

My sister Blanchefleur was very excited. She spent the whole day in my guest room in our grandparents' palace. To keep the trip to the impending ball at Bergfels Palace as short as possible, we spent a few days with Mama and Papa at their place.

Blanchefleur turned to Elsbeth, our chambermaid who had traveled with us. "Does she see this seam here? There is something wrong with it. Check this spot!" She clicked her tongue in displeasure. "And my cheeks are scarlet! No young gentleman will want to dance with me at the ball!"

She continued to complain as she turned back and forth in front of the large wall mirror.

She was constantly tugging at her evening dress and drove Elsbeth to despair with her choice of clothes. I, on the other hand, found it hard to concentrate on the French novel I was translating.

"You can really see every wrinkle in this mirror. It is really unflattering. I do not know what our grandmother finds so beautiful about it. When I look at myself in it, every little flaw comes to light."

Once invited to a gathering hosted by the Archbishop of Sens, whose hall was lined with more than fifty mirrors, our grandparents were enthused about these mirrors, whose frames were made of gold, silver, or ivory. They had acquired some magnificent pieces, one of which adorned the guest room.

It was rumored that the French king was green with envy and was planning an entire hall of mirrors for his palace. Of course, it had to be bigger and more beautiful than the archbishop's.

He was even more displeased that my grandparents had beaten him to it and purchased some of the most valuable and highest quality crystal mirrors.

"Chère Maman, please tell Ernestine to hurry!" my sister shouted at the top of her lungs. "Otherwise, she will make us miss the first dance at the ball."

Mama rushed up and I involuntarily hunched my shoulders in the face of the thunderstorm that followed.

"Ernestine! *Incroyable!* Simply unbelievable! This child sits around calmly and pretends to be a scholar! That is not proper for a young woman your age."

A shadow fell over the paper. Mama had stepped behind me, and when she saw the lines I had just written, she let out a short scream.

"Not only are you addicted to reading, but you are also picking up a pen yourself! I am speechless. I will ask your father, the Count, to consult our personal physician. After all, there must be a medicine that will put you on the right path and teach you how to behave in a manner befitting your origins." She stood in front of me and shielded the daylight with her figure. "And please look at me when I talk to you!"

I looked up at her unwillingly.

"Instead of sitting in front of these written sheets and straining your eyes, think about how you are going to dress! All the noble families from the surrounding area will be attending and I want you to stand out amongst the nubile young women. Even if you are promised to the most illustrious Crown Prince Baldrich, I want him to see how much all the other hand-some young men desire you."

"But, Mother, I am no longer a little girl." The fact that she had to bring up that damned crown prince made me even more upset. I did not want to think about him.

"It's all the more incomprehensible to me that the marriage was not accomplished long ago. You are old enough. You are seventeen!"

As if this conversation was not sufficiently unpleasant enough, my sister intervened. "What do you think, Ernestine? May I accompany you as maid of honor on the wedding procession to the palace?"

"That would be quite appropriate," Mama replied, joining my sister. "I think your dear father should push for a wedding soon. Otherwise, the royal family might change their minds."

I had to restrain myself from exclaiming, *Yes, please, I would not object to that!* Instead, I seized the moment and quickly sent dear Elsbeth out to get me some fresh water to wash my face.

"I just cannot decide," Blanchefleur continued to moan, alternately stroking the fabric of two dresses that she had laid out on my bed. The rustling of the fine silk fabric almost drove me angry. If she carried on like this, she could damage the fine embroidery.

"Blanchefleur, take this delicate, cream-colored ball gown. It emphasizes your virginity perfectly." As soon as she finished, Mama came back to my desk and took my head in her hands. She eyed me critically and tugged at my short hair.

"Ernestine, you need help with the hairpieces. It should be a dainty updo. It is a shame that you refuse to grow long hair! And the count supports you in your attitude, too."

"Mother, you know as well as I do that most of our friends and acquaintances have practically no hair left on their heads because of the heavy wigs. It is more practical this way."

Mama puffed. "If only you wore the hairpieces!"

Our chambermaid coughed.

"Madame?" She stood in the doorway with the wash bowl in her hands and looked at me. She hesitated, but I firmly waved her in. It would be a shame if she spilled the luxurious water.

"Elsbeth, what on earth is this *lavoir* for? I will not allow my daughters to come into contact with water that fills their heads with vapors. The very thought that germs could penetrate their pores during washing and make them ill... Ugh!"

"Mother, leave it alone. I've asked Elsbeth for it and I am only going to wet my face a little. Writing has made me hot. A little cooling before I apply the powder will do me good."

I nodded encouragingly to Elsbeth and pointed to the dresser where she should put the bowl down. Mama backed away from her as if she was carrying a poisonous substance.

"Even Louis XIV washes his face, hands, and mouth every day after getting up, so what could be so wrong with that?" I added in defense.

"This is not France, nor the court of the *Sun King,* young lady. Even though you are marrying an heir to the throne, that does not mean you can do whatever you like." Mama looked me up and down with contempt. "And do not dare go to the stables after changing into your ball gown!"

How did she know I was going to check on the horses?

My mare, Libelle, had been laming since the ride here. I had not wanted to miss the ride, as I hated the jolting in the stuffy and uncomfortable carriage. Hannes, the groom accompanying us, had mixed up a special healing ointment for Libelle's fetters as soon as we arrived, but unfortunately, it had had little affect so far.

I could not go to a ball and enjoy myself without first making sure that Libelle was well looked after.

"You have given me another headache," Mama complained. "Where has the violet ointment gone? I need to dab some on my temples."

And Mama rushed off.

"Er-nes-tine!" Blanchefleur suddenly stood next to me, her hands on her hips. "You will put on your ball gown, immediately!" She stamped her foot.

Sighing, I put the quill aside and weighed down the precious Basel paper, of which I had brought a small pile from home, with a bronze horse figurine. It resembled my mare Libelle.

Grandmother had undoubtedly wanted to make me happy with it and had it placed in the guest room, as she knew of my love for miniature sculptures!

I ran to the dresser, dipped my hands in the bowl, and moistened my face with a little water.

If only this day was already over!

***

Three hours later, we got out of the coach a little exhausted. I would have loved to have done without the unpleasant odor in the coach. I would much rather have ridden like my brothers, Count

Cuno and Count Humbert, and enjoyed the fresh air.

The sight of Bergfels Palace took my breath away. Built predominantly from mottled sandstone, it lay in the middle of an imposing garden whose size could only be guessed at.

"That was an incredible ride in the best weather and look what a majestic spectacle it is!" exclaimed Cuno, who joined us with Humbert in tow. "Look, dear sister Ernestine, there's the marble courtyard that was reported on in the *Freytags* newspaper."

I had to admit, the whole area offered a magnificent panorama: the arriving guests, all dressed in affluent robes. The many noble horses in front of luxury carriages, which drove to a side building and queued in front of the stables...

I had firmly resolved to let the event pass me by indifferently and uncaringly. I did not plan to waste a thought on the fact that this ornamental building would be my home soon. I had often heard that Crown Prince Baldrich was considering marriage to another and intended to oppose it. I could not believe that a prince would take me, a countess, as his wife.

I wondered why the king had once agreed to my father's proposal, as it would mean a considerable loss of prestige if his son married me. There were plenty of princesses who would surely be all too happy to take my place.

I would indulge in two or three dances with the crown prince if I had to. Papa had told me that the royal family had hired first-class musicians from London. As the last notes faded, I would dance inconspicuously into a corner. Afterwards, I planned to retire to one of the many rooms. There were supposedly eighty of them in addition to the two large halls.

Cuno had raved to me many times about playing cards with his friends. I did not want to miss the opportunity to peek over their shoulders and pick up a few tricks. Perhaps I could use them with the horse groomers in the stables, where I spent many evenings in secret.

At some point, my parents and Blanchefleur must have had enough of the dancing and chatter and wanted to make their way back. Then it was time to say goodbye to the palace, and hopefully never see it again.

Agatha

The daylight was reflected by the mirrors on the inside walls of the large ballroom and illuminated the room right up to the farthest corners. I could not get enough of the precious, colorful, velvety gowns of the invited ladies and wistfully suppressed the emerging desire to jump up and ask one of them, quite indecently, to dance. I was seeing many of the young women for the very first time.

My sisters—Benedicta and Marie Sophie—and I had spent most of our childhood and youth in the city palaces. But our father, the king, decided that we should join our brother, Crown Prince Baldrich, at Bergfels Palace. After decades of construction, it was finally habitable.

Baldrich's marriage to his betrothed was to be officially announced in the foreseeable future. And the wedding celebrations were due to take place within the next year. Marie Sophie, Benedicta, and I were instructed to *peu à peu,* little by little—make friends with the young Countess Ernestine, the multilingual, tempestuous Amazon who, according to hearsay, had been promised to my brother since childhood.

My sisters and I were to familiarize her with life at our royal court. An almost impossible task when I considered the differences in status.

I could not explain what had possessed my father to marry my brother off to a simple countess. Here, at Bergfels Palace, the newly-weds were to make their home and provide as many offspring as possible to ensure the succession to the throne.

The greeting to the count and his family was very stiff. There was no warm welcome from my parents, as I would have expected, and not, in my opinion, the way it was appropriate for the future daughter-in-law.

Several other noble families and representatives from distant states stood jostling behind the count and his entourage, also waiting to finally be received by us.

I lost sight of Ernestine and her sister, Blanchefleur, before I'd even had a chance to look at them properly or speak with them.

After the welcoming ceremony, our esteemed parents opened the dance. Soon afterwards, my brother asked a true beauty in a cream-colored gown to float across the dance floor with him, using rehearsed, ornate words. He seemed to be completely at one with her.

I narrowed my eyes and regretted not having my thread loop spectacles with me. The young woman had been introduced to me, hadn't she? That is right, it was the Countess Blanchefleur, the sister of the marriage candidate. But should Baldrich not ask his future bride to dance? Mama would surely intervene soon. It could all too easily be interpreted as an affront to Countess Ernestine if he continued to dance so eagerly with her younger sister.

His posture spoke more than a thousand words, and he beamed at his dance partner with his broadest smile.

Did he really like her? Or was it just a tactic to show how much he was against the marriage? That he did not care who he danced with?

Hadn't he signaled before the ball that he would retire to the smoking room as soon as possible to talk about hunting and play cards with his best friends, and Counts Cuno and Humbert?

On the other hand, it would be more than convenient for me if he were the center of attention today and attracted our mother's displeasure.

Then all eyes would be on him, and Mama would be distracted. She would not be able to give me persistent glances and gesture to me that I should present myself to Prince Rorich, for whom she thought I would make an excellent match, and stroll in front of him.

As soon as Baldrich had given his vows, she wanted to marry me off—it was high time, given my not-so-young age—to Prince Rorich, who was fond of all kinds of jewels and spices. In other words, everything that ladies usually loved. The prince who obviously preferred the company of my brother, Prince Cuno, or other young men.

I could not imagine living with him in his castle and giving him children. Especially not with my gynecological condition, which made me feel very uncomfortable and was getting to me, but for which our personal physician had not yet found a cure. Apart from that, I was enough for myself and could do without the eternally scurrying companions around me who did not share any of my leisure activities.

I gratefully accepted a cup of tea handed to me by a lady-in-waiting and enjoyed the hustle and bustle from my cushioned armchair.

"Agatha, come quickly! Join us!" Marie Sophie called out as she ran towards me in quick strides. Her cheeks were glowing, and she waved a fan frantically to catch her breath. "The musicians are about to play for us sisters. A *Rigaudon à quatre danseurs!*"

A mocking remark was on the tip of my tongue, as there were only three of us and the dance was designated for four dancers. However, my sister pointed her velvet glove in Benedicta's direction and at the young woman standing next to her. An hour ago, I had met her in person for the first time and had shaken her hand in greeting: Countess Ernestine!

"You are surprised, aren't you? I have already familiarized myself intimately with our brother's future wife."

I could imagine Marie Sophie sticking her tongue out at me from behind the fan. She always knew how to cleverly hide such silly gestures from bystanders and appear well-mannered to the guests. The young woman in question seemed to hear Marie Sophie's words and looked over at us. She approached with cautious steps, apparently not used to walking on the slippery dance floor. She bowed deeply to me, so deeply that I was afraid she might fall over.

"Your Highness," the young countess almost whispered. Marie Sophie pulled her up and made a startling gesture with her hand. "It is quite all right; you have already been introduced to my sister." Marie Sophie sighed. "Agatha, get up! Otherwise, you do not need an extra invitation."

That was true. Right after *jeu de paume,* tennis, fencing, and horse riding, dancing was at the top of my list of passions. I motioned to my lady-in-waiting to take my teacup.

Oos and *ahhs* rang out as I stood up and walked to the middle of the ballroom with my sisters and the enchanting-looking Ernestine.

Everyone who had been dancing up to that moment stepped aside and formed a small lane to the center of the hall. I watched expectant expressions; the assembled nobility eagerly awaited our dancing skills. They all whispered, the ladies behind their fans and the gentlemen behind their hands as I walked past them. I hesitated for a moment and spoke sotto voce to Marie Sophie. "Shall the Crown Prince not ask Countess Ernestine to dance first?"

"You can see that our brother's heart is fully focused on Countess Blanchefleur. Countess Ernestine has assured me that she does not mind if he dances with her sister." The countess nodded eagerly, so apparently, I had done the etiquette justice.

Marie Sophie, Benedicta, Ernestine, and I lined up and waited for the musicians to play the first bars. They finally started performing and I almost missed my cue. Countess Ernestine was transformed from the first note. Albeit she had initially looked unhappy in her ball gown and made an awkward impression, she now pranced across the floor with ease and gracefully turned her hands.

Funnily enough, I had to make an effort to remember the dance steps I was usually so familiar with: *Balancé* to the right, *Balancé* to the left, *Pas de Rigaudon,* land on three, turn to the side, open arms...

As a passionate dancer, I was truly out of time!

When Benedicta and I turned around and danced with our backs to Marie Sophie and Countess Ernestine, Benedicta gave me a questioning look: my intense study of the young countess had obviously not gone unnoticed by her. But we were already whirling back again and had to be careful to stay in time and not jump on the spectators' feet as the crowd pressed ever closer and closer.

As soon as we found the right beat and the right pose, I looked up and my eyes met Ernestine's. She winked and her lips seemed to boldly whisper the order of the steps to me. But that was no longer necessary. I even combined two particularly beautiful, but also difficult steps that the private teachers from the dance academy had once drilled into us and which I had remembered after my initial difficulties.

I dared to lift my skirts a little more than necessary, so that the outward position of my feet in the elegant shoes with silver buckles and small red heels was demonstrated to its best advantage.

After we had been dancing for at least one hour, my lady-in-waiting and my brother, Prince Baldrich, gave us a courteous hand signal that the musicians needed a break. So, my sisters and I went to my library with the young countess. I had it furnished in the style of the salon of an acquaintance, the novelist Madame de Scudéry.

Ernestine and I immediately got to chatting. Unceremoniously, we were on a first name basis and exchanged pleasantries as if the dancing had spun a bond between us. Artificial polite phrases or a rebuke on my part—albeit appropriate to my status—would have been out of place here, in my understanding.

Benedicta and Marie Sophie left for the garden after a while, and I went through the bookshelves with Ernestine. A book about keeping hunting dogs caught her attention and I told her about Mimi, my cute and funny little dog.

"Where is it?"

"My mother did not want to see her today. She commanded me to lock Mimi in my apartment because she growls at every stranger and can be quite snappy at times."

"It would be fun to have her among us!" Ernestine exclaimed. "Oh, can you show me Mimi afterwards?" I solemnly promised her that I would introduce her to Mimi in good time and invited her to sit with me on a bench. Instantly, she told me about her mare, Libelle, and her family's horse breeding.

"You would be amazed if you saw my brother's horses. If you'd like, I can tell Baldrich that you would be very happy to have one of the Berber horses for your wedding!"

"I would rather have a Spanish Karster mare," Ernestine replied with a thin lip.

"I am sure that should not be difficult," I assured her, although I did not understand why she had raised an objection against a beautiful Berber.

"Please forgive me, but I would like to go back inside. I'm feeling a bit dizzy as I have not eaten since lunchtime," she apologized and got up from the bench.

"Did I say something wrong?" I followed her example and stood up, too. "But you are right! You should be talking to my brother, not me."

"No! It is not because of you. Can I confess something to you? And you will not tell anyone else?"

I raised my hand as if to swear an oath and nodded.

"I do not get anything out of this marriage. I only have one consolation: that you are such a nice person, that we both get on so well, and will see each other every day..."

I decided not to say anything in response. And my stomach was growling so loudly at that moment that I was sure it could be heard all the way to the farthest room in the palace.

"Let us go back. I could do with a bite to eat as well."

We walked silently back into the ballroom where the footmen were lighting countless candles. The chandeliers illuminated the hall, making it look more festive than ever. Many guests had retreated to the adjoining halls, where food and drinks were being served, or gaming tables were being set up. Only a few dancers remained on the dance floor.

Among them was my brother, who glided across the parquet with Countess Blanchefleur in a vigorous Allemande.

Ernestine and I gave each other a meaningful look before we went into one of the other rooms and sat down at one of the generously laid tables to fortify ourselves.

Chapter Three

Ernestine

Lost in thought, I sat at my desk and stared at the gilded leather wallpaper on which a lightly clad Artemis, playing the lyre, and her favorite companion, Callisto, were emblazoned, surrounded by nymphs and animals of the forest. Artemis bore a certain resemblance to Agatha. Except that I had encountered her body covered in expensive fabric.

Yes, Agatha.

Since our time at the ball, I had simply called her Agatha and not by her title. We had been so familiar with each other in conversation, and she hadn't reprimanded me once about it either.

I did not dare imagine her with so little light fabric around her body. At least not during the day. I should leave such fantasies to the night. I felt the blood rush to my ears and focused on the wallpaper again. Artemis' bow and arrows were leaning against a tree trunk. A true idyll. And I could really put myself in Callisto's shoes.

Oh, goddesses, I wish I could swap places with you! Such a carefree life free from constraints.

I felt the urge to write to Agatha again, even though I had already handed a letter to her through the emissary earlier that morning.

So far, she had been very vague about my request to pay me and my family a courtesy visit at Sturmstein Castle. But I definitely had to see her again!

I wanted to show her my horses, books, and a portrait of myself and tell her so many important things that could not be conveyed through words. When I held the pen in my hand, I sometimes did not know how to organize my thoughts and feelings and put them down on paper.

But today I had the certainty that my pleas, which I had made to her in countless letters, had finally been heard. I looked at the fine, precious paper in my hand and gently stroked her lines, unable to get enough of her curved handwriting. Her letters were always several pages long. She told me anecdotes about life at court and the funny pranks her little dog, Mimi, played on her.

"Countess?" Elsbeth stood in the doorway. "Your parents are calling for you and your sister."

***

Blanchefleur and I stood upright next to the mantelpiece in the drawing room and kept silent, full of tension. We waited for our parents, not wanting to sit down. Finally, the heavy wooden door was opened by a servant, and our parents entered. The steward, the concierge, the lady of the house, the head cook, and a few other servants followed them. They stood at a proper distance from our parents.

Our brothers, Cuno and Humbert, were also present. Still in their riding clothes, they must have been summoned directly from the morning hunt, which underlined the importance of this meeting.

Normally, they were informed of news directly by Papa in his private quarters. Papa nodded encouragingly to the group and then to Mama.

"Ernestine, Blanchefleur, you would not believe what distinguished guest is paying us a visit!" Mama clapped her hands happily and Papa twirled his beard with a satisfied expression on his face. "Dearest daughters, have a seat," he politely requested of us, pointing to two armchairs he had recently purchased. We immediately rushed to the new furniture and carefully took a seat.

Mama and Papa also sat down; the more expensive, fabric-covered chairs were reserved for them. I remembered the ball at the palace, where King Casimir and Queen Coletta had sat on chairs just like these. However, they were even more noble than ours, as their fabrics were interwoven with gold and silver threads. Cuno and Humbert stood next to our parents and looked at our father expectantly.

"Her Serene Highness Princess Agatha will pay a courtesy visit to her soon-to-be sister-in-law and her family," Mama revealed before Papa could even get a word out. A murmur went through the servants.

"The most powerful King Casimir himself has written to us that he will send his dear daughter to us," inserted Papa, "so that she can get an impression of the parental home of his soon-to-be daughter-in-law for him."

My parents were indeed flattered. Blanchefleur leaned over to me. "Why does Prince Baldrich not come himself?" she whispered, and I sensed disappointment in her voice. "I wish the Crown Prince would at least escort the princess so that he could look around in person."

And yet Agatha undoubtedly only came here because of me. If only Blanchefleur knew! The last letter I had received from the princess that morning said it in no uncertain terms:

> *Illustrious Countess Ernestine, dear friend, it is quite explicitly a private visit, which I personally,* en personne, *will make solely for your sake.*
>
> *I need three rooms to myself, where I can retreat to at times, because I cannot think of anything to talk about with your parents. Also, I must freely admit—please forgive me—that the difference in class gives me a headache. Then again, I will not be able to get enough of your company...*
>
> *In addition, my two chambermaids and the lady-in-waiting who will accompany me need a place to sleep close to me. The coachman will certainly find a place to rest with your grooms.*

"Ernestine, you and Blanchefleur have to help me with the preparations. I cannot manage the whole arrangement on my own," Mama continued eagerly. "It will be useful for yourself later on, if you have to act as a person who does the inviting."

Then, she turned to the concierge. "Neville? Princess Agatha is to stay in our best rooms. He will check her chambers and have them prepared for our honorable guest."

"Of course, *madame.*"

"We should ask our cook to bake a fancy cake," I suggested, and my sister nodded eagerly.

"Oh yes, a cake with redcurrant jam as a filling, with spices and almonds."

Mama looked questioningly at our cook.

"Ah, the *Linzer Torte,* a good idea," she agreed with a smile. "If I may suggest: You, illustrious countess, must offer coffee as a side drink." The lady of the house immediately added, "I will have the most beautiful saucers served for it."

"But we cannot just serve cake." Mama looked around, perplexed.

"I know a few excellent recipes from a famous Leipzig chef, for example, chicken with pistachios and asparagus, followed by a *Marzipan soup* as a starter," the cook explained.

"Mmm, delicious," Blanchefleur and I exclaimed, and our mother beamed with enthusiasm.

An idea came to me, but I hesitated for a moment, before saying, "Well... At the ball, tea was served to the princess."

"But, Ernestine, we do not want to follow every new fashion." Papa shook his head. "Besides, the price of that drink is too high, and we do not have the financial means of a royal family."

He bowed to Mama. "I see, dearest, that you will be very busy from now on. I do not think you need my help in these matters. If you will excuse me, I have business to attend to."

Papa grinned and disappeared with our brothers in tow. Our mother immediately returned to the arrangements. Rarely had I been in such a good mood when planning a guest visit with my mother and Blanchefleur as I was that afternoon.

Chapter Four

Agatha

I allowed a suitable amount of time to pass after the ball before announcing my visit to the Count's family and my friend Ernestine. *Yes, I already referred to her as my friend.*

Although we had only met at the ball and had not seen each other since, innumerable letters had been piling up on my desk ever since. Each one was more flattering than the last and none of them were of a nasty, mean kind. They were all upright and honest, full of trust in me that I would not reveal their contents.

I decided that it was no longer appropriate to refuse Countess Ernestine's invitations. Besides, I was literally drawn to the young woman who could dance so brilliantly, chatted cheerfully and sincerely in her letters, did not mince her words, and whose views on life were similar to my own.

Of course, I took the trip on the pretext of getting to know the young Countess's parents' house and reporting back to my brother. It had not taken much persuasion to convince father of the importance of the visit.

I decided to take only two chambermaids and a lady-in-waiting with me on the trip. This kept the costs down and the Count and Countess did not have to worry about how to accommodate a whole entourage of crowned heads.

Besides, I had heard that some of the rooms at Sturmstein Castle were in a terrible state!

***

Three weeks later, I wandered through Ernestine's room to look at a painting she had repeatedly praised from all sides.

"A beautiful portrait. How old were you then?" Ernestine had been excellently depicted. The portrait seemed almost three-dimensional and gave the impression that the young woman, who was gazing brightly out of a window, could step out of the frame at any moment. Her décolleté dress was lavishly decorated with brocade embroidery. It literally besotted me.

And it was not just the dress and the brushstrokes—no, I was all the more fascinated by Ernestine, who radiated an incomparable calm and yet seemed curious. My friend had not promised too much in her letters.

"I received it a year ago for my sixteenth birthday." There was pride in her excited voice. "Pretty, isn't it? Papa and I visited my aunt in Paris last year. He really wanted the daughter of a former master student of Lavinia Fontana to paint a picture of me to commemorate the visit."

I winced at the name Fontana. She had been known to use ancient sculptures as models for her work, and in her last known painting she had depicted the naked Minerva getting dressed. I immediately had the goddess in mind as she looked directly at the observer. I wondered if Ernestine resembled her in this naked costume.

Oh dear, I had to think of something else!

"Mother almost fainted when she heard how expensive the artwork was." Ernestine giggled. "When she saw this painting of mine, she demanded that our father return it and reclaim the fee. But he refused because he liked the portrait."

No doubt it was not only the cost of the work, I estimated, but also its artist, who did not please the Countess's mother. Nonetheless, I said, "I do not think so. What justification is there for not wanting to keep the painting?" Her daughter looked as courteous and pretty in the painting as any mother could yearn for.

Ernestine gave me a mocking look.

"As if you do not see it yourself! Mama complains that I am not pale enough. But I have spent a lot of time outside, at the stable, helping to break in horses. So, it is inevitable that I will get a bit of a tan. I do not like this exaggerated powdering anyway."

I looked in the large wall mirror and felt ashamed of my pale skin, which suddenly seemed far too light.

I really should use less face whitener. But I love the rose water mixed with the lead white. It smells so nice! I could not do without it.

"She does not like my short hair at all either," Ernestine continued unperturbed. "The paintress should have portrayed me with my hair pinned up or at least with curls, which are very much in the height of fashion now. You know, hair put into a thousand little curls, just like Louis XIV's mistress appeared at one of his latest balls. Mama says I look like one of those women who were supposed to end up on the scaffold with their hair cut short. I looked terribly disfigured and unfeminine in the painting and was also depicted much older than I actually was at the time the portrait was taken."

At that moment, a long strand of hair slipped in front of my face, and I hurried to tuck it in-conspicuously behind my ear.

"I do not have hair as beautiful and healthy as yours, which is worth growing long." The young Countess must have seen my gesture, and her remark flattered me immensely.

"I can be styled with my own hair and rarely use wigs or artificial hairpieces," I confided to her. "Although, I have nothing against wigs if they are scented with lavender."

Ernestine wrinkled her nose, and I wished I had said something negative about wigs. Especially as I liked this short coiffure on her much more than the artificial hairpieces she had worn at the ball. She looked a little cheeky and could easily pass for a young man with the right clothes. Although, to be honest, I had never met such a beautiful young man before.

"What is more, the portrait is flawed, as there is no piece of jewelry crowning my décolleté or head," she continued cheerfully. "My mother wanted at least the pearl jewelry that my great-aunt—God rest her soul—had bequeathed to me to be added afterwards. But I hardly ever wear jewelry. It just annoys me and gets in the way of everything I do. And I do not like showing it off in front of our servants."

"I think you look really enchanting. The paintress captured you perfectly. There is nothing missing." Did my voice tremble a little? "And short hair seems to be very much in fashion in France. I am utterly convinced it will not be long before more and more women get rid of their heavy long hair."

"The paintress said the same thing. She was thrilled and incessantly stroked my short hair." Ernestine's cheeks glowed. "I think she was trying to make advances to me."

This intimate remark gave me a little sting. A paintress making advances to a countess? What could this lady be imagining? It was not appropriate for a service contractor to approach a young countess with indecent thoughts. Although Lavinia Fontana had been a virtuoso in the field of painting, this did not elevate her to a higher status—let alone the daughter of one of her pupils!

I suppressed my rising anger and asked as impassively as possible, "So, did you respond to her flattery?"

"How could I? Papa, of course, insisted that one of my cousins who lives in Paris attend the sessions." That calmed me down a little.

"Why did your father not have Mary Beale draw you? She is the best portrait paintress I know."

Ernestine sat down on a scissor chair and slid back and forth, embarrassed.

"Papa could not afford that," she said quietly.

Oh dear, I had put my foot in my mouth again. I felt like my clumsy little dog Mimi! I refrained from saying that Mrs. Beale also had assistants who were excellent with a paintbrush and whose work was reasonably priced.

"Would you not like to sit down too?" Ernes-tine pointed to a beautifully crafted armchair decorated with carvings. I immediately recognized that the piece of furniture came from a family of craftsmen known to our royal family, who had been purveyors to our court for decades. I sat down gratefully, and Ernestine continued the conversation.

"You would never guess what is going on in faraway Paris."

"You have never been there before?"

"No. It was my first and probably my last trip abroad, if Mama and Papa have their way."

"What did you see?"

"Well, we went to see a ballet at the opera. It was not just any ballet, because for the very first time, a woman was actually dancing on stage."

"Ah, let me guess, the wonderful Mademoiselle De Lafontaine, a true queen of dance."

"Yes, exactly! And I had an invitation to a literary salon in the Marais where Madame de Scudéry was reading from her ten-volume adventure novel. It was packed, I have only ever seen so many people at balls. The atmosphere was very relaxed, everyone was joking, and so terribly nice, intelligent, and well-read."

This information did not come as a surprise to me. For I knew from my dear brother Baldrich that Ernestine had appeared in Madeleine de Scudéry's salon on the very evening that he had stayed there in disguise with his friend Prince Rorich. Of those present, only Madeleine had been in on it.

Just like me, Baldrich often attended events in costume so as not to attract attention. He had left the soiree early for fear that Ernestine might recognize him. This, in turn, had saddened Madeleine greatly, as I learned from her letter shortly afterwards: *Why did your dear brother beat a hasty retreat after only two hours?*

Ernestine jumped up and adjusted the curtain in front of a window—stroked a cushion here, moved a vase there. On the one hand, she looked young and fragile, but on the other, she radiated a great deal of self-confidence during our conversation.

Her behavior was interesting, and it gave me a sudden nervousness that I couldn't explain. I followed her movements. She was so beautiful.

"I would have wished to have traveled back from Paris through Rome." Her words snapped me out of my reverie. "I would have loved to see the Palazzo

Farnese, where Christina, the former Swedish Queen, lives. She is so brave, refusing to marry her whole life! Do you know what they're claiming she said?"

Although I knew exactly what she wanted to say, I shook my head. I wanted to hear it from Ernestine.

"'I could not bear to be used by a man the way a peasant uses his fields, she is said to have said. And grandmama told me that the former Swedish Queen once showed herself in male attire in Brussels!"

"Well, well!" I winked at Ernestine with mock indignation. She smiled at me, and for a moment, time seemed to stand still.

"Christina was a role model for me." I openly expressed what had been on my mind for a long time, but which I could not tell any of my ladies-in-waiting or court ladies. "I wish I could be as vehemently against marriage as she was. What harm could come of it? I would not even miss out on the throne, as it is entitled to Crown Prince Baldrich!"

"I always thought I was the only female who preferred pantaloons to skirts." Ernestine beamed. "They're so practical for working in the stables and horse riding. I do not understand why we dames should cover ourselves in such heavy fabrics." Suddenly, she stood in front of me, and I felt as if she wanted to touch my arm.

"I am not sure." Shrugging my shoulders, I stood up in awe of her proximity and walked to the window. An idea came into my mind.

"Do you love the theater? I know an interesting play that you would really enjoy."

"But please do not let it be from Molière." Ernestine snorted.

"What do you have against him?" Curious, I searched her facial features for an answer.

"Mama loves the *Comédie Française* and I have had to read some of Molière's works to her so often that I almost know them by heart."

"I was thinking of a play called, wait, *Le Mariage forcé, a forced marriage?"*

"*The Forced Marriag*e? From Molière after all!"

"No, not from Molière, let me think. I mean an enforced marriage; the play is called *The Forc'd Marriage.* It was written by a woman, by Aphra..."

"...Behn! I've heard of her."

"She sees marriage as a form of prostitution for financial reasons."

"And you think we could see the play in a theater somewhere near here?" Ernestine's brow furrowed skeptically.

"Of course not. We would have to travel to Paris or London for that."

"I do not think Papa will let me; I was only in Paris with him last year. He and Mama think I have seen enough of the world. Besides, traveling is so expensive, and he does not want to spend so much money on his daughters. The dowry alone takes up a lot of financial resources."

Unaffected, I made a gesture of refusal. "Who says he has to pay for the trip?"

Ernestine stood there thunderstruck, and I was afraid she might even faint.

"You would pay for a trip for me? But is that even feasible?"

"We will see," I replied noncommittally. As Princess and sister of the Crown Prince, it was my privilege to make sure that Ernestine did not get bored or even fall into melancholy. After all, she was due to give birth to a healthy prince forthwith. What could be better than going on a trip?

If I did it cleverly and the royal personal physician accompanied us, then Papa would spare neither expense nor effort and would have no objection to a little trip. I was sure of that.

My thirst for action took hold of me as I headed for the room door elatedly. "Did you not want to show me the rose garden?"

Chapter Five

Agatha

I enjoyed my time at Sturmstein Castle immensely. I have more than positive memories of the warm welcome I received in the Count's family household. Apparently, they had not taken offense at my parents' brusque welcome at the ball or cleverly concealed their disappointment.

During my stay, I almost forgot that I was not at the royal court. Time seemed to disappear. I wanted for nothing, and the food was excellent. After my return to Bergfels Palace, I arranged for an emissary to present Countess Ernestine with a gold taler and a small, but complete, collection of coins as a token of my appreciation and gratitude for her hospitality.

I had written the word *friendship* in the accompanying letter in particularly beautiful German *kurrent* writing.

To my annoyance, Mimi had jumped around my feet in such a way that the paper had sailed onto the floor in my fright. Then, the little animal had left a small paw print on the paper. I had added a note as a P.S. saying that Mimi simply could not wait to meet Ernestine soon and that she was sending her warm greetings with this little work of art.

I missed Ernestine immensely, was no longer enough for myself and, with increasing consideration, felt that an invitation in return was entirely appropriate. Was that not what Mama wanted from me? That I would finally join the recent round of visits, invitations, and return visits of the nobilities?

As a result, I decided to organize a small courtyard concert in the late summer of that year. Not a big performance, but a nice soiree in an intimate circle, which I was able to manage from my budget.

This meant I could decide whom I invited and that I did not have to take into account too many conventions or the convenience and ideas of the King and Queen or even my brother.

***

None of my few closest friends wanted to miss the concert. Decency and etiquette constrained me to invite Mama, Papa, and my siblings. But Benedicta was visiting a cousin, and I knew from my father and Baldrich that they detested afternoon music occasions that served as a pastime for chattering women. So only Mama and Marie Sophie kept us company.

To my great delight, Ernestine had set off alone with Blanchefleur, accompanied only by two chambermaids. I had written to her parents assuring them that I would provide them with two maids and two companions at court so they would be well looked after during their short stay with us.

I knew that Ernestine would love the lively, cheerful *Capriccio Ueber das Henner und Hanner-geschreÿ,* a *Capriccio About Hens and Roosters cackling happily,* in which the hens and roosters were imitated excellently. And indeed: during the performance, after the first few notes, she tapped her foot lively to the beat and occasionally laughed out loud.

The recorder concert had barely finished, and the applause had died down when Ernestine stood up and tugged on my arm, pulling me out of my chair and spinning me around in circles. We went faster and faster, and I let myself be infected by her joy and had a great time.

"Agatha, what an unconventional, funny piece of music you have chosen! I have heard a lot of Poglietti's compositions, and I know one or two organ pieces, but that he has written such a wonderful, humorous piece..." The words bubbled out of my friend, full of enthusiasm.

A loud cough could be heard, Mama did not seem to take the young countess's exuberance as happily as I did.

"Princess Agatha, it was a pleasure to be able to attend this wonderful concert." My mother pushed her way between us. "It is unfortunate that your father is unavoidably involved in political business." As soon as she had finished, she turned to Ernestine, who had moved a few steps away and was standing off to the side with her sister, looking rather lost.

I looked around, but my other friends were all gathered around the players of the flute quartet and were not paying any attention to us.

"Dearest Countesses, you are welcome to join me later in the small gallery and dine with me and my daughters," Mama invited my guests. "King Casimir has promised that he will not miss the opportunity to visit us later in the evening."

She looked at Marie Sophie and me with a piercing gaze.

"In the meantime, Princesses Agatha and Marie Sophie will show you to Countess Ernestine's prospective chambers. Dearest Agatha, please make sure that Crown Prince Baldrich can spend a few minutes alone with his bride-to-be and exchange a few words with her."

While Mama spoke to my sister and me, she looked Ernestine over from head to toe. Her eyelid twitched, which was an unmistakable sign of her displeasure. Ernestine's hairpiece was a little askew and she was wearing almost no powder.

I had to get the two Countesses out of here as quickly as possible to prevent Mother from embarrassing the lovely Ernestine with an ill-tempered remark in front of everyone. Because, unfortunately, Mama loved to tease.

I also had other plans for the evening after the concert. Even though we could not refuse dinner for the sake of politeness, I wanted to spend as much time alone with my guests as possible.

"Ernestine, Blanchefleur," I addressed the two young women, "please follow me. We will go through the east wing—it's the shortest way."

Without further ado, I received an indignant look from my mother. "Child, you're not going to ask our guests to walk through the long corridors. That's not worthy of a future queen, is it, Countess Ernestine?" She emphasized the word countess.

"The servant had better not stand here looking so bored. The young ladies need a *portechaise* in a hurry," she ordered one of the servants standing in the corridor.

While we waited for the sedan chairs, I said goodbye to my other friends and asked the ladies-in-waiting to accompany them out and leave us alone with the countesses.

When the servants came forward with the carrying chairs, Ernestine and Blanchefleur were visibly uncomfortable getting into the sedan chairs. Had they ever been carried in a *portechaise* before? I did not remember seeing any at Sturmstein Castle. There, we had walked everywhere on foot.

***

We had only just reached the rooms of the Crown Prince's future bride when Ernestine and Blanchefleur jumped out of the carrying chairs. The torchbearer accompanying us was quick-witted enough to dart to the side, otherwise Ernestine would have scorched the sleeve of her dress on the lamp. I made sure that they were served cider as a refreshment.

But it was not a servant who brought the wine—no, it was my brother Baldrich himself. He rushed over from somewhere and was not too shy to offer the young women the drink.

I was annoyed that he first handed Blanchefleur a glass before turning to Ernestine. *What rude discourtesy toward her!*

What was more, he and Blanchefleur chatted like old friends and ignored us sisters to the best of their ability.

Ernestine, on the other hand, did not seem to mind at all. Instead, she tugged on my sleeve and whispered to me, "Let us leave the two of them alone. They seem to have a lot to talk about, even though they write to each other several times a day."

This was news to me. How could my brother withhold something like this from me and keep secrets from me? It seemed that not even the fawning courtiers knew about it, because then I would have found out from my chambermaid.

"Come with me, I will show you the little library I have had set up for you. The idea came to me after my visit to Sturmstein Castle and our pleasant and informative conversations about books. There are not many yet, but I have gathered a small, exquisite collection of good literature."

I spontaneously linked arms with her, undoubtedly still under the impression of the chatting siblings and the correspondence that had remained hidden from me until then.

Ernestine let it happen, and I felt as if she was even leaning against me a little. So, the two of us walked to the library and I showed her the beautifully bound works. Soon we were sitting close together—I on a simple, velvet-covered chair with a backrest, as I had left Ernestine the beautiful one with armrests and gold brocade embroidery. Book after book was piled up on two small tables that we had pulled up. We sat there with our heads together and did not want to stop chatting!

A chambermaid brought us little Mimi, who showed her very best side. She greeted Ernestine happily—even gave her paws and never left her side.

Ernestine also stayed with me when we went to my chambers after dinner, and I changed my clothes for the night. She accompanied me to the smaller bedchamber, as the bed in the alcove was more comfortable than the free-standing bed in the magnificent but oversized bedroom.

Mimi made herself comfortable at our feet. It was still warm outside, so we left the windows open and could listen to the swallows chasing insects.

The intimacy we felt was balm for our souls. I persuaded Ernestine to take off the artificial hairpiece and kept stroking her short hair. She allowed me to call her *Stinchen* and we hugged and kissed each other without shyness. We fell into a deep sleep long after darkness had set in.

Chapter Six

Ernestine

In winter, our family spent a lot of time at my grandparents' prestigious country estate. This palace, where we had also lived at the time of the ball, was only an hour away from the nearest town, so our provisions were secure. The servants did not have to travel long distances for shopping and errands.

When the weather permitted, Mama and Blanchefleur visited close friends and relatives, while I usually preferred to go to the nunnery's library and study the abundance of old writings there.

The bookmistress knew how to keep me constantly provided with new literature. Through her, I made the acquaintance of several other female translators who stayed at her convent from time to time.

However, snowstorms and freezing rain had been alternating for three weeks and Papa had forbidden us to go into town. The carriage ride was too dangerous. So, it got a bit tedious from time to time. I could not write letters to Agatha from morning till night or devote myself to my translations—it was too exhausting.

Therefore, Blanchefleur and I were glad of any change. We had heard that a sealed envelope from the King had been delivered to our father and that he intended to discuss its contents with Mama. We immediately rushed to the library and listened at the heavy door. My heart was pounding as I heard Papa's words through the door.

"Dearest, the Royal Family could not have chosen a better match than our daughter. His Serene Highness, our most illustrious King Casimir, had already expressed this in the warmest terms in private after the last hunt with our mutual friend, the Prince of Unterwald. In his letter today, the King insists that the marriage should take place this winter for tactical and geopolitical reasons."

"Absolutely not!"

Mama's voice shrilled through the room, but Papa drowned her out. "And, of course, I will not deny him his wish."

"Otto! How can you..."

"My dearest, first you wanted our firstborn to be married soon, and now you are against it?"

"I want a big celebration, and that is not possible in winter. The aristocracy would only be even more outraged by the improper marriage of a Crown Prince and a Countess! I'd love to know what the Queen thinks of her husband's idea, as it is about her family's reputation."

"Oh, dearest, you must be joking. Are you seriously going to refuse the King's request?" Papa laughed, but his voice sounded threatening as he continued: "The marriage must be worth a lot to His Serene Highness King Casimir, otherwise he would hardly send a courier in this uncomfortable and cold weather."

"Poor man," Mama said. "He should have the cook give him some hot soup."

"Do not distract yourself, dear. What do we care about the courier? He will be used to such circumstances," said Papa. "Besides, we cannot afford to delay the marriage!"

"Pah, you have not been in a hurry to do that yet at all."

"At last, we could part with the cost-intensive land east of the border that we once agreed in writing as a dowry for the christening of our lovely Ernestine Philippa. In this vein, we would get rid of its costly cultivation," continued Father. "This is an appropriate dowry for our eldest, as King Casimir said in his letter. He emphasized that the additional acquisition would strengthen his position. Particularly in relation to the Kingdom of Bohemia and the Archduke of Austria, who was driven by ambitious reform programs. Incidentally, the King would gain more respect from his subjects if he also owned this part of the land."

"You have it good! I wish I were in your place." Blanchefleur laid her head on my shoulder and sighed softly.

I remained silent while Father became all the louder behind the door. "King Casimir has generously entrusted me with the administration of the estates, which he believes I have looked after excellently so far..."

"But..."

"...and which he had inspected and valued *incognito* by various experts last summer. There is even a rumor among my friends that the King is considering elevating my humble self to the rank of Prince, which would increase the value of my remaining possessions immensely!" he concluded at the top of his voice. He probably wanted the whole castle to know how *formidable,* how great he was, in the King's eyes. Well, that way we did not have to press our ears so hard against the door.

"The most gracious Princess Agatha also reported to the King that during her stay with us she had felt as if she were at the Court of the *Sun King* and that our family was truly worthy not only of the title of Count, but also of the title of Prince."

"It is unreasonable for Prince Baldrich to make the journey to our castle in the depths of winter," Mama interjected, returning to the actual subject.

"As far as that is concerned, he does not have to make the journey to us..."

"We cannot expect Ernestine to walk through the snow either!" Mama became increasingly indignant. "It's too dangerous, and robbers would have an easy time of it. I do not even want to think about her having an accident with the carriage."

Papa snorted dismissively. "Oh no, not at all. Who is talking about that? The marriage will simply be performed *per procurationem,* by proxy marriage, as a glove marriage."

Shocked, I listened to my father's words.

On my fifteenth birthday, he had promised me that I had nothing to fear, and that the marriage would not take place so soon. His words today, however, went against this word of honor.

I had foolishly believed Papa's promise and hoped that the chalice of marriage would somehow pass me by if only enough time passed. That the Prince would definitely meet and prefer a much more suitable wife, a Princess.

As if! Worse still, the Crown Prince had been very rude and dismissive towards me when we first met at the ball. So, I had given in to the hope that he, too, was opposed to an imminent marriage.

And then there were the secret letters he wrote to Blanchefleur! Conversely, she also seemed to adore and like him very much.

My sister clawed at me. Did she know that I was about to storm into the room and scream at my father in rage? I almost did not care whether that was appropriate for a countess or not.

Mama's statements, on the other hand, surprised me. Until recently, she had never expressed any reservations about this unequal union. She had been the driving force and had wanted to bask in the glory of the Royal House.

"Ask the chambermaid to order the glove maker here this week, bad weather or not. We will commission a fine pair of gloves, preferably interwoven with gold embroidery." Papa's patronizing tone displeased me. "We will then give these to our youngest son Humbert to present to the Royal Family. It will do him good to go through snowstorms and freezing cold and stand his ground. I dislike his conceited demeanor. Sometimes I think he is not my son with the way he behaves."

An awkward silence followed and Blanchefleur looked at me questioningly.

As far as I know, Mama had had a younger admirer for a while, the brother of the Prince of Unterwald. But I thought they only met rarely and in the presence of their families.

"What are you implying?" Mama was outraged when she found her tongue again, but Papa ignored her shout.

"On the ride, Humbert should show that he can master difficult situations," our father continued. "As far as I am concerned, you can send a letter to the Queen and ask her to arrange a festivity or a small ball for our daughter next summer. Tell her that you would like this very much as a token of appreciation for Ernestine and our family. Well, you know how it should be put in letters."

My face must have gone white as a sheet at that moment.

At least I will not need to apply any more powder today.

My father wanted my brother to say yes on my behalf in front of Prince Baldrich.

No! Never!

I strongly agreed with Mama's opinion that a proper marriage ceremony should only be held in the summer. She had to talk Papa out of this crude idea of a glove marriage. This would buy me time, because apparently there was only one way to avoid getting married: to escape from Sturmstein Castle and the life that was becoming more and more repugnant to me.

I had to build up another, more independent one. One where I had earned my own loaf of bread at the end of the day after the work was done. By working honestly and with my own hands. And once I had enough money and my own little hut, I would bring Agatha and Mimi to live with me. Because it seemed to me that deep down, my friend was just as unhappy with her life as I was.

I had been working on an alternative solution for a long time and it was not for nothing that I tried to get on well with our servants, my chambermaid, and the grooms. When the day of the wedding approached, I would take the bundle I had deposited in the tack room, throw myself into the knee breeches of a groom, and set off on my escape with Libelle.

I must stall for time, I thought. At least until the weather has improved and the roads have been cleared of ice.

***

I was lucky, because the glove maker was down with a very bad cold. So, I was able to take care of everything that seemed important to me before my escape from Sturmstein Castle. Above all, I had a letter to write.

Agatha's visit, how much she had praised my portrait, the court concert that followed, and how much we had to say and tell each other—all of this bewildered me.

I did not have much time, though, and it was unthinkable to write directly to Agatha and tell her about my escape.

I had to make it look as if my lines were intended for Prince Baldrich. I would explain myself in it—reveal that I could not become his wife and that my heart belonged to his sister. Would he show the letter to his sister and make her aware of my deep love for her?

I sat down at my desk and reached for my writing utensils. I quickly let the quill glide over the paper.

> *Most Serene Prince Baldrich, au sujet de votre soeur, regarding your sister, the most gracious Princess Agatha: She is a good soul and has shed tears with me...*

I silently read the letter for the last time, in which I described how we both had recited a moving love poem by heart during her visit and how we had been overcome with emotion.

> *...and because of my sadness...*

Emotions welled up inside me and I dabbed my eyes. The candle flickered and I cursed. My hand trembled and I suddenly found it difficult to add a clean and legible note with my quill without spilling ink.

> *The good Princess Agatha has shown me all her kindness, so much so that I love her abundantly.*

Again and again, I paused. Was it appropriate to send a confidential letter to the Crown Prince? At least this time it was a good thing that I was considered to be his wife-to-be—it would not be noticed if he received a letter from me, would it?

Could I trust him freely? I would have loved to tell him more—like the kiss Agatha and I had exchanged recently. But I should keep that to myself, if only to avoid putting Agatha in need for explaining herself to her family and getting into *malaises*, into trouble. She was certainly in for an interrogation.

Chapter Seven

Agatha

"Your Highness, are you absolutely sure?" With raised eyebrows, the chambermaid took me out of my musings. She let one of my long strands of hair slip through her fingers and shook her head disapprovingly.

"Did I not make myself clear?" I replied impatiently. "One lock will certainly not be enough. Cut out enough of my hair so that it can be woven into a pretty piece of jewelry." I had not forgotten Ernestine's praise of my hair. I wanted her to enjoy it, too, and remember me forever.

"But, Princess, why do you not take one of the many silver bracelets and give it to the Countess?" intervened one of the two ladies-in-waiting who were—on my mother's orders—always present when I was getting dressed. The older I got, the more I detested this custom.

I regretted telling her about my plans. Without any discussion, I wanted to give this very piece of jewelry to Ernestine as a sign of my loyalty and love for her. I had gotten the idea from the lines of the poet Opitz, who had once written about a bracelet woven from his beloved's hair.

"No, I do not want any more objections. Please proceed." I resolutely closed my eyes for a moment to prevent any further interference.

After what felt like an eternity, the chambermaid put the scissors to work and cut off a beautiful long strand of my curly locks. She then presented the strand of hair to me before putting it in a small box. By a hairsbreadth—what an appropriate term—she almost stepped on Mimi's paws.

As a lady-in-waiting sitting by the window told me, a messenger from our court jeweler was already waiting outside. I always found it exciting to know who was coming in and out of the palace, whether suppliers were arriving with their carts or guests were arriving for Papa. Or whether emissaries were riding out into the distance with urgent letters from my father, as happened two weeks ago.

A chambermaid had happened to be a witness when Papa had asked our scribe for advice on how he could politely and stylishly, but vehemently, communicate a matter of great importance to Count Otto.

Ernestine's name had also supposedly been mentioned. After asking my mother, I found out that our parents were now pushing for the marriage and wanted to hold it as soon as possible. Sadness had paralyzed me ever since.

"Your Highness, your brother, would like..." The valet did not get any further. Instead, Baldrich, who was standing just inside the door, drowned him out.

"Dearest sister Agatha, I would like to talk to you." Baldrich walked towards me with his arms outstretched. As he kissed my cheeks in greeting, the smell of alcohol hit my nose instead of his otherwise very pleasant-smelling perfume.

"Ladies, please," he addressed the court ladies, "I would like to speak to Princess Agatha in private for a while."

But they were not enthusiastic about his request and none of them made any effort to get up. Out of politeness to me, they waited for my approval. Sighing, I jumped to my brother's aid.

"The weather is so beautiful, the paths are no longer icy, and they are cleared of snow. Maybe you could just take a little walk through the garden and enjoy the sunshine that has been so rare lately?"

***

What my brother told me would send the whole kingdom into a state of shock, but the news was merely a balm for my downcast soul. Baldrich begged me to devise a plan with him so that he could say yes to Blanchefleur. He showed me a letter from Ernestine that he had just received from his valet. I was very touched by the familiar handwriting and the love for me that Stinchen revealed to him without restraint.

Baldrich assured me that he held Ernestine in such high esteem that he did not want her to marry him when he desired her sister. I had to acknowledge his courage. Nonetheless, I wanted to reassure myself.

"Are you serious? Are you even sober yet?"

After all, he had been playing cards with friends until late in the evening. If I believed my chambermaid, the young gentlemen had drunk a large part of the wine supplies, which had actually been intended for an upcoming banquet with high-ranking merchants from Venice and the Netherlands.

"I have never been so sure," Baldrich replied with a firm voice and a serious expression. "Blanchefleur is the most enchanting young woman I have ever met." He swallowed and coughed. "I feel sick. Can we open the window? I think I drank too much yesterday after all."

Reluctantly, I moved to the window and opened the heavy shutters. "Better?"

Baldrich had followed me, pushed aside one of my fine Chinese vases that was standing there, and leaned on the windowsill. He took a deep breath.

"It will be no easy task to convince the King and Queen that you would like to take Ernestine's younger sister as your wife. Not to mention the illustrious Count Otto and his true-hearted consort Walburga."

"I am well aware of that. To make matters worse, our parents are already displeased, as you are hardly likely to be Prince Rorich's chosen one."

"You have been informed by our parents?"

"A terrible story. I do not envy your fate," Baldrich confessed. "A woman who cannot bear children is worth nothing in this world."

I did not see it that way and was glad that Mama and Papa were finally satisfied with our personal physician's explication. After extensive studies on female nature and discussions with several scholars, he had come to the conclusion that I would not be able to have descendants due to a female complaint.

So, my parents stopped looking for a marriageable prince for me and concentrated on choosing suitable sovereigns or princes for my younger sisters. And if I succeeded in realizing Baldrich's wish, well, then I would have Ernestine all to myself.

"As for Blanchefleur..." my brother returned to the reason for the conversation.

"...thus, we have to hurry," I finished his sentence.

He looked at me in astonishment. "Why?"

"As I heard through Yolande, our esteemed father sent a messenger to Sturmstein Castle a fortnight ago. He is insisting that the wedding takes place as soon as possible. It would be best if you went to see Papa right away."

"What? Why do I not know about this? That can..." Baldrich's gagging interrupted his words abruptly and I held my hands in front of my face to avoid having to watch the Crown Prince relieve himself in one of my most beautiful porcelain vessels.

In this state, he was not capable to face our parents and make known of his most heartfelt wish, I realized angrily.

***

Occurrences came thick and fast over the next few days. Papa received a letter by a mounted courier from Count Otto, who proposed a marriage by proxy in order to conclude the desired union as quickly as possible.

Two accompanying letters came from Countess Walburga. Unlike her husband, she asked our mother in all seriousness to put in a good word with the King so the marriage—with a pompous celebration—would not take place until the following summer. Only then would Countess Ernestine be given the honor she deserved as the future wife of the Crown Prince.

The other letter, with the same content, was intended for Papa. Our father immediately had the countess's intercession burned in the fireplace.

He grumbled something along the lines of, "Since when do women determine the fate of the world?"

Mama, on the other hand, considered sending the countess at least a tactful reply in which she would talk her out of the *bizarre* idea and approve of a glove marriage.

That same evening, Baldrich revealed his love for Blanchefleur to our esteemed parents. Understandably, they initially refused his wish and were both appalled and full of indignation.

Papa asked for a moment of silence to think about the problem and came up with what he thought was an excellent solution.

"As expected, you will fulfill our wishes and those of the Count's family and marry Ernestine. But after all the festivities and when she—as planned—has given life to one or even two heirs and you reign yourself, no one will care if you make Blanchefleur your *maîtresse-en-titre,* your supreme royal mistress."

Papa strutted across the room and seemed to think he was very imaginative. "Blanchefleur would then be in possession of a semi-official position, which would even come with its own apartment in the Palace, where you could visit her legitimately whenever you wanted," he added with a triumphant look in our direction.

But to my relief, Baldrich was not satisfied with that. He hurled words of displeasure and expletives at Dad, which I did not even know he knew, and then went into his apartment. I ran after him, and we talked for a while.

"We still have a lot of convincing to do, but I have no doubt that the outcome will be good," I tried to comfort him.

Marie Sophie, who had returned from visiting a friend, joined us and I told her about what had happened. She in turn interrupted me after a few words and asked me to listen to her.

What she told me pulled the rug from under my feet: Ernestine had escaped from Sturmstein Castle!

Chapter Eight

Ernestine

My mare Libelle did not let the long distance she had already covered show. She carried me far from home without any noticeable sign of fatigue, despite the still rather chilly weather. It was not until the evening, when we had passed a few villages whose names I had never heard before, that I dared to allow us both a break at a small lake.

After praising Libelle highly for her stamina, I led her to the water so that she could drink. Hungry, I pounced on the apples that I had hastily stolen from a larder and tied up in a small bundle.

Sated for the time being, I tied my horse to a thin tree trunk and looked around. In the distance, I saw a wooden hut with smoke rising from the chimney. There was a small extension, probably a stable, as there were two cows and a horse in the adjoining pasture. Drapery and clothes were hanging on a line. Would I be allowed to stay in the stable for the night?

I looked down at myself. Did I look ordinary and poor enough in the knee breeches that Elsbeth had bought me, and I had put in the equestrian storage just in case? I ran my hands through my short hair and was glad that the cold wind had blown through it properly. Then I put on the linen cap that I had had the presence of mind to grab from the tack room that morning. Libelle snorted, and I went to her and untied her.

"Come on, my dear. Let's try our luck."

***

After the first night in the stable of the farmer's family, I heard roaring and howling in the morning.

"You belong to the lowest of the lowly servants, but even they are more disciplined than you and do not shy away from work!" the farmer shouted.

Before I could get up and see what had happened, the eldest daughter of the family ran to me in the stable. She was covered in tears and holding her cheek. Confidentially, she told me that she had not been up early enough and had not made a fire. Her mother had then scolded her, and her father had beaten her out of the door. I quickly realized that I should not stay here for long if I wanted to keep my life.

Above all, who could guarantee that the farmer would not push me around or even mistreat me at some point? Especially if, for what-ever reason, he found out that I was a woman! After all, he did not even shy away from violence with his own flesh and blood.

I comforted the girl as best I could, then packed the piece of bread I had received from the farmer's wife the night before into my bundle and set off again before sunrise.

I passed through countless small villages and was finally able to call a tiny little room my own in a small settlement in the early summer of 1683. It was right next to the church, which also ran an orphanage where young girls were taught reading, writing and arithmetic. They also received sewing lessons in preparation for working in a household.

The house master was looking for a young lad to help out. Since then, I had been looking after the garden and the chickens and doing minor repairs. I did not shy away from the work, but I kept my mouth shut because I did not want to give myself away.

More than once I mentally thanked the grooms and maids who had allowed me to look over their shoulders so many times and secretly lend them a hand at Sturmstein Castle, despite considerable protests.

Every day, I received a warm meal consisting of soup and vegetables, a slice of bread now and then and a small piece of meat once a week. I quickly got used to the modest life.

I came across a little stray dog, and it reminded me a lot of Mimi. I wondered if she comforted her owner well.

Chapter Nine

Agatha

In the summer of 1683, a good six months after Ernestine's escape, my brother took Countess Blanchefleur as his wife. I witnessed a pompous ceremony in the cathedral of the nearby town. The festivities that followed were supposed to last a total of five days. A royal monogram was presented to the public, in which the first two letters of Blanchefleur's and Baldrich's first names were artfully interwoven.

I was happy for the young couple, but among all the tears of joy shed by the relatives, I shed tears of sorrow and sadness, as I missed Stinchen so much. There were rumors about her whereabouts time and time again, but that was all I was allowed.

I had secretly entrusted three mounted messengers with the search for her. If they had to carry out an obligation for our father elsewhere, they were to keep an eye out for my beloved. I had secretly had two seals with similar monograms made for myself and Ernestine as a consolation, in the hope that we would meet again one day. In this case, I wanted to give her one of them for our correspondence.

Papa had gone to great expense for the wedding celebrations. They swallowed up a sum equivalent to his income for a whole year, and the costs were many times higher than the value of the dowry. The Count alone would not have been able to pay for it.

The church was lit with 1683 candles, one for each year of our era. On each day of the celebrations, there was a feast with all kinds of delicacies, including roast swan. My father insisted on three show dinners, at which only our royal family sat at the table.

Several rows of onlookers from the crowd of commoners stood around us and watched as we took the food in our hands and drank the finest wine from little silver cups.

An outdoor ballet was also performed, which the King and Queen initiated with tempered steps to the music of a Pavane.

The Crown Prince danced a round dance with his bride in the second act and I had to admit that they made a beautiful couple. Blanchefleur surprised the audience with a Sarabande to which she accompanied herself with castanets, and my brother lost his composure for a moment at the sight of her comeliness. Tears ran down the cheeks of all those present at this display of love.

The last evening ended with a big fireworks display. Even the crowd was invited to watch the spectacle in the sky and the adults were given free beer. Candied fruit was handed out to all the children and alms were given to the poorest of the poor.

The festivities were extremely harmonious, and everyone made an effort to be nice to each other and treat each other very tactfully. Ernestine was not mentioned at all.

Only a few expressions of displeasure were heard here and there that the prince had married beneath his dignity. It should at least have been a princess. But in general, joy prevailed.

I had instructed my ladies-in-waiting to keep an eye out for Stinchen among the revelers. I hoped so much that she would mingle with the people in disguise. But she had not been seen.

Chapter Ten

Ernestine

On one of my rare visits to the nearby town, where I bought new culottes and knee breeches, I heard the news that the military was looking for young men in the villages and settlements. The soldiers sent out did not even shy away from dragging boys and young men out of church services or breaking into houses. Terrible news!

I had thought I was safe for so long after my disappearance. No one questioned my appearance, as I made every effort to behave like a man and speak as little as possible. The tobacco I indulged in from time to time, which I had bought as medicine from the town pharmacy, made my voice sound rougher.

By now I had become accustomed to men's clothing, and it was inconceivable to me that I would ever wear ball gowns or robes of any kind again! But knowing about the military troops pouring out made me frightened. I should have guessed that I would not remain undetected forever and that my game of hide and seek would eventually be uncovered.

One fine morning, I was milking the goats in the stable when I heard hooves clattering in the yard of the poorhouse and orphanage. Unannounced visitors were unusual in the morning. Loud voices reached my ears.

"Hey, where is he?"

"We'll get him!"

Before I knew it, soldiers stormed into the stable and two of them roughly grabbed my arms.

"I knew there'd be a little boy hiding here," roared one of them. "Another renegade! How dare you evade the defense of the Motherland?"

They pulled me out and threw me into the courtyard. If I expected the other employees of the orphanage or some of the children to come to my aid, I was mistaken. Some of the helpers had their backs to me and were hanging up clothing, the old gardener was quietly digging in his beds, and a farmhand with a wooden leg was sweeping the side path to the church.

Nobody was interested in me and my looming fate.

***

I waited several days in the dungeon for my sentence, crammed in with all the other men who had been captured as renegades. I would not survive life imprisonment; thus I preferred to be executed by the sword. The food was moldy or so softly cooked that its components were no longer recognizable. There was no lavatory like at Sturmstein Castle, and the stench was unimaginable.

The warders were all uneducated, so I could not start a conversation with them and explain myself—let alone ask for a visit from a lawyer. If

I revealed myself as a woman to these simple men, I would have to fear being violated by them or my cellmates. As a result, I had no choice but to find other ways.

Finally, one Sunday, a priest came to hold service for us. I offered to pray the Latin responses to the priest's calls as an acolyte, as most of the other prisoners did not speak the language. I could hardly wait for the mass to end.

Afterwards, I asked him to hear my confession. I confessed that I was not a boy, but a woman. But how could he help me? He advised me to keep my disguise for the time being and wanted to consult with some church servants about how I could be freed from this bad situation.

I had not been particularly religious as a young girl and had previously avoided going to church on Sundays whenever possible, but now I was particularly devout and prayed for a rapid end to my misery. Under the pretext of hearing my confession again, the priest came to see me again a few days later.

He asked me a few religious questions. Some of them concerned the books of the convent I knew. However, I was in such poor physical shape due to the adverse conditions in the dungeon that I did not stumble over them. Nor did it occur to me to tell him about my noble origins.

When the day of the trial arrived and I was led into the courtroom in chains, I seemed to have lost my vision. Sitting in the front row of the audience was a nun who was the spitting image of my Agatha.

Now I have gone crazy!

Chapter Eleven

Agatha

It was to Ernestine's advantage that there was an equestrian postal connection from the oh-so-distant town whose inhabitants had treated my companion so unkindly.

The snorting of a horse in the echoing courtyard and Mimi's growling and barking had woken me up early that morning. Baldrich, who was traveling the borders of our country and meeting with envoys from foreign kingdoms, had sent me a mounted courier.

"May he speak now? What is so important that my dear brother is sending a mounted courier?" I interrupted the man, who kept babbling greetings.

"The Crown Prince suspects that Countess Ernestine works for an orphanage, Your Highness, and has now been captured."

The courier handed me a letter from my brother. "He asks you to make your way to him as quickly as possible. I have instructed the grooms to prepare one of the hunting carriages for you so that you can set off without delay."

The sentences were written down in a hurry, but luckily, I had often sat with my dear brother and supervised his homework. His scrawly handwriting was well known to me, and it did not take much effort to decipher it.

***

Baldrich had reason to believe that a renegade who had been picked up and arrested by soldiers in the stable of an orphanage was in fact Ernestine. After a long struggle, the priest had broken his vow of silence and told the sisters of a nunnery in the nearby convent about the strange but educated-looking woman who had told him about her fate.

According to him, she could recite the Ave Maria and Pater Noster fluently and flawlessly, without stuttering once. She also did not give the impression that she had grown up in a poor household.

Full of excitement, without paying any attention to the courier, I read Baldrich's lines aloud to myself:

> *"Furthermore, dear sister, she was said to be able to read and write and expressed herself in a refined manner. One of the nuns had asked the priest to ask the woman a few questions about certain books. Based on her answers, she is certain that the illustrious Ernestine is stuck in the dungeon. Only she could know about some of the precious documents kept in the convent."*

According to Baldrich, the nun made her suspicions known to the Prince of Unterwald, as she knew of his friendship with the Count's family. He had informed my brother immediately by mounted courier, as the military prisoners were to be put on trial in a week's time. With a pounding heart, I dropped the document.

"Good man, He really does bring good news, if the suspicions are correct." I thanked the courier before turning to my chambermaid.

"I will be on my way immediately. Please gather the bare necessities for me in a small bag and forward it to me by courier."

Chapter Twelve

Ernestine

Again and again, I asked Agatha to tell me about the incidents from the time of her journey in the hunting carriage. I could not get enough of the story of how she had set out to help me out of my predicament. Blanchefleur and Agatha's sisters also hung on her every word.

"I stayed in the city mansion of the Prince of Unterwald, so it was only a short walk to court," Agatha remembered again. "It was also his idea that I should show up there in the monastic habit of the Order of the Nuns so as not to attract attention."

"I was surprised when I found out on the morning of the trial that I would have a lawyer at my side." I shook my head in disbelief and could hardly believe my luck. From now on, I was allowed to live at court as Agatha's lady-in-waiting.

Little Mimi jumped up and down—the animal was out of her mind about me. She got on really well with the little dog, who had been tracked down by a hunter and brought to me some time after I had told Agatha about the little stray.

How happy the animal was to see me again! I quickly dropped a few crumbs down and they pounced on them, yapping happily.

"Baldrich had instructed our family's lawyer to support you and save you from a prison sentence or worse," Blanchefleur intervened in the conversation. "I will be eternally grateful to him for that." She stroked her belly reassuringly, which had already taken on considerable proportions. Soon, she would make me an aunt. "Sister dearest, tell me... I heard you lost consciousness in the middle of the trial?"

"Fortunately, for Ernestine, that was extremely helpful for her." Agatha smiled at me.

"I knew there was something wrong with the nun sitting in the front row. She looked familiar, but I could not place her at first."

"When she finally looked me in the eye, she fainted at the realization. Did I intimidate you that much?"

"Not that. The military judges alone made me uncomfortable, but then... you..."

"I was worried about your health because you looked very thin in the rags you were wearing. Nevertheless, it was an advantage that you displayed this uncharacteristically ladylike behavior there."

Blanchefleur looked questioningly from Agatha to me and back again.

"The military judges had no choice but to admit that the alleged young boy and renegade was actually a woman. For when Ernestine sank down onto the cold floor, her torn shirt pushed up and revealed one of her breasts. So, they could all see with their own eyes that the lawyer had only spoken the truth with his claim that Ernestine was a woman."

Blanchefleur and Agatha's sisters snorted with laughter.

"A murmur went through the hall, and everyone present shouted in confusion and the chief judge had trouble calling everyone back to order." Agatha sighed. "I immediately ran to Ernestine and covered her body with my veil to protect her from the eyes of the others."

"When I regained consciousness, the verdict was given in my favor so quickly that I begged Agatha to pinch me very hard a few times afterward. I have rarely been as relieved in my life as I was on that day."

"As women have no place in a war, Ernestine is not a potential soldier. So of course, she is not considered a renegade..."

"...and the military judges unanimously agreed to release me from imprisonment," I finished.

Blanchefleur turned to me. "Now, tell us. How did you find out that my dearest Baldrich was successful in his courtship of me?"

"I heard in one of the Sunday sermons that the Royal Family had made Crown Prince Baldrich's engagement to you public. Believe me, I was overjoyed for you," I affirmed. "For the first time since my escape, I deeply regretted being so far away from Bergfels Palace. Otherwise, I would have dared to watch the lively celebrations in my disguise and mingle with the people to catch a glimpse of you pretty couple."

"I wish my dear husband Baldrich had been able to convince the King and Queen and our parents more quickly to take me as his wife instead of you. Then you could have spared yourself the escape and Agatha much suffering for your well-being." Blanchefleur sounded reproachful. "How worried we were!"

"Yes, there should be a way to get letters and messages on their way more quickly."

"We should be able to fly like birds."

"Or simply breed faster horses."

"A carriage that uses some kind of apparatus to help the horses pull and accelerate all by itself, as if by magic." All the sisters were talking excitedly.

"I do not think even the fastest mounted courier could have stopped Ernestine from escaping." The wise words were spoken by Agatha.

"But now I am with you, and I am not going anywhere," I confirmed in a firm voice.

Chapter Thirteen

Thirty years later, in 1712

Ernestine

The carriage slows down and comes to an abrupt halt. The attendant and the coachman consult each other, but I do not understand a word. I lean forward to the flap at the front and push it aside.

"Why are we stopping?"

"One of the horses is lame. We cannot continue like this. We need a replacement horse. I suggest that..."

With a cough, the attendant, whom my brother has chosen to accompany me, interrupts the coachman. "Countess, not far from here is the city mansion of the Prince of Unterwald. I would strongly advise you to spend the night there. Tomorrow, after a good break-fast, we will continue our journey, God willing, with a fresh carriage horse."

"That would be best, yes," confirms the coachman.

Should I really put up with another night? The plan was to reach a village on the edge of the Bergfels region by dusk, spend the night there, and then travel the last three hours to the castle in the morning.

But in the current situation, what else can I do but give in? Besides, the Prince of Unterwald is a very tolerant man who is well-disposed toward me. I am sure he will offer me a place to stay for the night straight away. His stables also enjoy an excellent reputation. The grooms are all very skilled and our horses would be well looked after there.

How long will it take me to span the remaining distance? The city mansion is halfway there. Agatha once mentioned that it was a good forty kilometers from there to the Palace. Of course, we would have to make an extra stopover in the carriage to give the horses a rest.

Unless... Another thought flashes through my mind, but I keep it to myself and agree with them.

"All right, I accept the proposal."

***

Far too much time passes before the attendant returns with a replacement horse for the carriage from the Prince of Unterwald. I immediately realize that the attendant has also swapped his horse. It looks fresh and strong. *With this steed, I can get to the Palace in no time,* I think to myself.

If I want to see Agatha alive, I have to act now. I walk purposefully towards the attendant and reach for the reins.

"Please dismount for a moment," I ask him in a resolute voice and pat the black horse on the neck. "I want to have a look at the horse. It is a very beautiful animal." The young man looks a little uncertainly at the coachman.

"The countess is a real horse expert—do her a favor. I need some time anyway to unharness the lame horse and bridle the one you have brought here," says the coachman and the attendant obeys.

I do not know where I get the strength from, but I pull up my skirts, put my foot in the stirrup, and swing myself onto the horse after a hop or two. My knees almost do not twitch and my back stays still, I realize with satisfaction.

"But, madam, how can you..." the attendant begins, but there is no time for hours of discussion.

"I do not care whether you like it or not. I am on my way," I reply. "Coachman, can he tell me the quickest way to the Palace?"

He complies and tells me which direction to take. After a few kilometers I could take a shortcut that we could not take with the carriage.

"Please make sure that the lame horse is well looked after by the Prince of Unterwald and thank him for providing me with this beautiful black horse." With this final instruction, I urge the animal on and do not give my companions another glance.

***

After hours of cross-country riding, my horse slows down and suddenly stops, snorting loudly. I dismount and give him a good talking to. I encourage him to take a few more steps, but he has no strength left.

I must have been wrong about this animal's stamina.

I throw my head back in despair.

Has everything conspired against me?

It is unthinkable to continue torturing the poor animal. I have to leave it to its fate and move on foot quickly.

I hope Agatha has not already left this world. But a deep feeling tells me that she is waiting for me. Once I reach the lands of the Palace, I will send a groom to the animal so it can be returned to the Prince of Unterwald.

After a few meters, I have enough of the bulky skirts. I pull them up to below the knee and tie the ends together so that they do not keep getting caught in the bushes and undergrowth.

Soon, I can see the little river that belongs to the village of Bergfels and the fork in the road that I am so familiar with—the one that has a path leading up to the Palace.

I have almost made it! Even if I certainly no longer look presentable.

I look down at myself. The once precious fabric of my shoes is tattered, and I free my feet from them since they are no longer worth anything. Barefoot, I run to the heavy portal, the gravel digging into my soles.

Chapter Fourteen

Agatha

I should be grateful to have had such a truthful companion as Ernestine at my side. If she does not make it here in my lifetime, then it will have been good.

And yet, my now weak heart pines for her so much. My sister, Benedicta, claims that my close relationship with Ernestine is the reason for my illness. For God punishes the wicked through physical suffering.

What is more, my illness is a holy instrument to chastise me and lead me on the right path. But as I can never, ever let go of Ernes-tine, there is no cure in sight.

I forgive Stinchen for leaving so quickly and I do not want to leave this world while in a quarrel. Later, she will probably realize how unnecessary our dispute was.

I would like to give in and leave her a few lines. I would like to reassure her that I am at peace with her. Then, she will be at peace.

Nevertheless, I am too weak to put a single syllable on paper. I have to wait until Marie Sophie rushes to my side so that I can dictate the lines to her. She is the only one I trust to pass on my words to Stinchen.

I wish I had had a miniature portrait made of Ernestine. The one where she is wearing the décolleté dress with the brocade embroidery. Then I would always have her with me and could have the piece of jewelry buried close to my heart.

As I was pondering, I missed our personal physician, Doctor Helande, entering the room. With Marie Sophie and my chambermaid in tow.

Oh no, not another bloodletting. And in the daytime!

Even though I have told him several times that it should only be done by moonlight. I know it has to be done, but I am always so weak afterward. In fact, my eyes close immediately after the treatment, despite my best efforts to stay awake.

I cannot help but think back to the time when my Ernestine was on the run and fell into the net of the soldier recruiters...

The smell of porridge, enriched with leek and milk and warmed up, wakes me up. Yolande praises the food in the most beautiful tones, trying to make the light food palatable. Despite her efforts, I immediately feel sick.

"No, not the porridge," I moan, exhausted. Yolande holds another plate under my nose, but I do not have an appetite. Even the figs in almond milk she offers me do not tempt me. "I do not want to eat any more."

"Shush!" My chambermaid dabs my lips with a wet cloth.

Oh, if only it were Ernestine! Where is she?

***

Suddenly, there is a babble of voices and a commotion in the corridors outside. The door is torn open, and my maid calls out, "Can you not see your feet are bleeding? And why do you look like that? You cannot go to my mistress like that!"

The personal physician is also protesting vehemently. "You must not disturb her under any circumstances. The Princess needs the utmost peace and quiet!"

My body is too weak to get up, but I know only one person would dare to come to me in such a state.

It can only be her—my Ernestine!

"Stinchen?" I whisper and I can already smell her perfume at my side and feel her embrace. A whole sea of tears of relief runs down my cheeks and I am not at all ashamed of them.

"Agatha, please forgive me for leaving you. Such a stupid disagreement."

"It was my fault," I answer her. Or is that just what I think? The dispute about our letters, which were to be burned at my request, and her rebellion about it... I should not have been so hard on her! But now she is back.

"I will stay by your side forever." She wipes the tears from my face and a thought flashes through my mind.

"Yolande? That..."

"...Gift!" she adds, and once again she surprises me with her quick thinking.

Sometimes it seems to me that she can read my mind, even though she is just a chambermaid. She hands my faithful friend a wooden box decorated with mother-of-pearl. Now is the right time to leave it to Ernestine—in all our years together, I had never found the right moment to give it to her.

When Stinchen holds the bracelet made from my locks of hair in her hand, she starts to cry. But she quickly calms down and kisses me on the forehead out of sheer gratitude.

Shortly afterward, I hear a rustling sound. My vision is blurred, but I can clearly hear Yolande's words: "Wait, Countess, here is the opening. Look how beautiful it looks on your wrist."

"Agatha!" Stinchen says to me after a moment of silence. "What did I hear from the servants as soon as I entered Bergfels Palace? You refuse to eat? You must eat a little something to regain your strength. Then you can attend the summer ball in a few weeks and enjoy the dances with me."

Ernestine's childlike enthusiasm makes me smile. I certainly will not be dancing another step in the ballroom, and she knows that too.

Should I ask for a mandolin player? A little music might lift my gloomy mood. I remember the little concert of hens and roosters that I once organized and that Stinchen liked so much. I laugh briefly, but I can hardly inhale, and it must sound like a croak.

It takes a while before I can breathe in and out properly again. I drift off into sweet dreams and suddenly I am whirling across the floor with Ernestine again, suddenly starting to float...

Epilogue

In 1722

Ernestine

It still makes my chest hurt like hell when I put on this precious bracelet, woven from a strand of Agatha's hair as a sign of her loyalty and love. She passed away ten years ago and left me this piece of jewelry. Thanks to her care, I also have a collection of coins and a total of three pieces of gold, which I received from her over the course of our time together, full of love and affection.

I am reluctant to destroy our correspondence, her letters to me, but will have to in the future. They comfort me in many difficult and lonely hours. Our disagreement about this immediately comes to mind. After Agatha's death, in Marie Sophie's presence, Yolande handed me some carefully tied-up parcels containing our correspondence with a mysterious expression.

It was Agatha's last wish to keep at least some of our correspondence in a safe place. I will deposit a few of the letters, as well as the seals with our monogram, in the archives of the Palace and the Castle. A very special one I have hidden inside the walls of the Castle.

Will the children of my siblings one day discover the paper and read the lines? Hopefully future generations will be spared being told whom to marry. I hope they will be able to live in freedom, without any constraints, and that they will be able to provide for their own well-being.

I miss Agatha. It would be a pleasure to tell her what is said to have happened two years ago: Allegedly, a woman in men's clothing had to stand trial for fornication with a woman.

Unbelievably, Agatha and I were not the only women who shared a bed and could not imagine a life without each other!

But the two ladies from the simplest of circles were so permissive that fate was not as kind to them as it was to us. One of them was even sentenced to death and the other was imprisoned for the rest of her life. My dearest Agatha was extremely clever and had done well to hire me as her lady-in-waiting.

Loud children's laughter and dogs barking pull me out of my grief. My nieces and nephews come running up, followed by a spaniel that looks very much like Mimi—God rest her soul.

"Great Aunt Ernestine, come out into the garden and play with us!"

I stow the bracelet safely back in the mother-of-pearl box and immediately join Blanchefleur and Baldrich's children's children.

Acknowledgments

Writing a historical novelette set around the 17th century is no easy task. Although this is a fictional story, I wanted to make the events as real as possible!

My heartfelt thanks go to all my first readers—my wife, Petra, as well as Uschi, Sandra W., and Stefanie, Senta Herrmann, my German editor, and Sierra Campbell, who did the English editing and eliminated false friends. Your comments and remarks, suggestions for inconsistencies, corrections and critical questioning, especially with regard to historical facts, were extremely helpful and I am once again amazed at how this coherent novelette emerged from vague initial ideas!

Dear readers,

If you would like to read more about the later inhabitants of Bergfels Palace or find out how the love letter hidden by Countess Ernestine came to light centuries later, then I recommend the stories *Christmas at Bergfels Palace* and *A Date with Castle Ruins.*

I am also currently working on creating a website where my readers can see all my books at a glimpse.

If you enjoyed *A Truthful Companion By My Side,* I would be delighted to receive a review on one of the typical portals, however short it may be.

Contact: Claudine-Auteur@web.de

Also published by Claudia Haase:

What's Christmas Without Walnut Cookies?
Paperback: ISBN-13: 9783756844487
E-Book: ISBN-13: 9783756870721

Christmas at Bergfels Palace
Paperback: ISBN-13: 9783757829438
E-Book: ISBN-13: 9783758386732

A Date with Castle Ruins
Paperback: ISBN-13: 9783757887940
E-Book: ISBN-13: 9783758380860

Also by Claudia Haase
(in German language)

Published by BoD:

Walnussplätzchen unterm Weihnachtsbaum
Booklet, ISBN-13: 9783751995269
E-Book: ISBN-13: 9783752632729

Athena and Murina
Booklet, ISBN-13: 9783752605129
E-Book: ISBN-13: 9783752697162

Weihnachten im Schloss
Paperback, ISBN-13: 9783754346938
E-Book: ISBN-13: 9783755703143

Rendezvous mit einer Burgruine
Paperback: ISBN-13: 9783756839650
E-Book: ISBN-13: 9783756880690

Published by MAIN Verlag:

Einspruch zwecklos. (K)eine Schwalbe zur Untermiete
Paperback: ISBN: 9783959496940
E-Book: ISBN: 9783959496933